The Girl Child Ordeal
(Adesuwa)

Patrick Ijiekhuamhen

Copyright @ 2022

Table of Content

CHAPTER ONE

THE BIRTH OF ADESUWA

Once upon a time in the ancient city of Benin, Edo State, a child was born to the Enoma family; her name was called Adesuwa meaning "Born in affluence". Mr Enoma the father was a farmer known all over for his commercial farming in Yam and Cocoa. While the mum deals on petty trading.

Adesuwa was a favoured child by the gods but this was unknown to the parents and other members of the community "a canal mind they say do not understand the things of the spirit". The birth of Adesuwa brought friends and well-wisher to the Enoma's compound. White powder was rubbed on the face, chest and palm of all the guest as a sign of celebration, guest were entertain with the native black soup and pounded yam served hot with a bottle of Palm Wine as it was indeed a festive period for the entire Enoma family. A lot of gift rolled in for the baby in the form of clothes, bathing soap, powder as well as other gifts for the mother.

During the celebration, Mr. Enoma managed to smile all through to friends and well-wishers but deep down within him he was not a happy man because he always prayed to the gods to give him a male child as his first fruit. The emergence of a female child shocked Mr. Enoma that led to sudden hatred for Adesuwa, as he often regard her as a curse to his family rather than a blessing. Afiangbe, the mother of Adesuwa often try to encourage the husband with soft words that he should allow the wish and aspiration of the gods be done. She pleaded severally saying "Ọdor mwen n'uwa" let the wish of the gods be done, worry not". Inspite of the incessant plea to move on by Afiangbe to Enoma, he still allowed the issue to weigh him down.

Inspite of the prevailing circumstances and issues in the family surrounding the birth of Adesuwa, she grew in health, strength and beauty. Adesuwa was loved by everyone that comes across her, her smile was soft and left dear memories to all those that came in contact with her. Mr. Enoma kept Adesuwa far from him and he never showed that fatherly love as expected.

Years rolled by and Adesuwa became three years old and the dad was still mean to her to the extent that he did not enroll her for school. Other kids that celebrated same three years birthday with her were beautifully dressed on their school uniforms waving at Adesuwa going to school, tears rolled down her eyes wondering why the world is not fair to her. Adesuwa at age three summoned courage and approached her mum asking critical questions regarding why she was not in school, she begged for answers. Afiangbe as usual encouraged her daughter not to worry and be strong that she would speak to the dad to enroll her for school the next year.

Afiangbe came again begging the husband to show their daughter some love by ensuring she gets what is due to her which is quality education. Mr Enoma responded, keep quiet woman and don't repeat this matter to my hearing again.Afiangbe decided to change tactics by preparing the favourite meal of her husband which is black soup and bush meat prepared hot with pounded yam "there is a popular saying that the way to a man's heart is through the stomach".

Mr. Enoma after eating the delicious meal slept and woke up and started to consider the wife's plea for allowing their only daughter go to school.

CHAPTER TWO

ADESUWA GO TO SCHOOL

The next year when it's time for enrollment Mr. Enoma offered to pay only Adesuwa fees that he will not spend any other penny. He acclaimed and lamented "Female children are nothing, but a male child will continue my lineage and bear my name from one generation to another". Afiangbe encourage the husband once more saying female child is as good as males, she acclaimed "my husband one day I know the gods will change your perception about female children, I know you will regret someday the way you are treating our beloved daughter Adesuwa".

Afiangbe took the school fees money and raise some extra cash from her petty trade to make up the balance for school uniform, sandals, school bag and books for her daughter to begin schooling.

Adesuwa upon seeing the mother from afar ran to her saying "mummy oyoyo" meaning mummy welcome and they both came inside together happily. As they entered into the room, the mum displayed the things she bought on the bed, the school uniforms, socks, sandals, books as well as receipts for school fees payment. She said with all joy "my daughter your dreams of going to school has come to reality you are resuming Monday next week".

By Monday, Adesuwa beautifully dressed was set for school, she went to her mum to confirm how she look, the mum replied you look awesome my daughter. The mum got dressed too and escorted her to school and handed her over to the head master of the school named Mr. Okosun.

Adesuwa resumed school full of enthusiasm as she frequently answered questions asked by her teachers, she also asked key questions to get better clarification on subjects not clear to her; most of the teachers were astonished by her brilliance. Afiangbe visited her school on a faithful day while she was in class to request from the teachers how her daughter was doing. The first teacher said "I love the composure of your daughter Adesuwa" second teacher "Adesuwa follows you while you teach and she is always the first to indicate to answer questions raised" third teacher "Adesuwa your daughter is a brilliant student". After receiving all these responses, Afiangbe broke into tears "full of joy" after all her efforts were not in vein and the daughter did not put her to shame for convincing the husband.

Afiangbe return home, called the daughter "Adesuwa" she answered mama I'm on my way, and when Adesuwa came the mum told her to continue the hard work that she was in her school today and all the reports she gathered about her were very nice. When Mr. Enoma returned home from the days farming activities, he was a little bit tired requested for water to bath. The wife gave him his usual hot water to bath and after bathing, he grabbed a class of palm wine to relax and wait for his food.

Afiangbe came out dancing and singing in front of the husband, Mr. Enoma was flabbergasted as it has been long she saw his wife in this mood. He responded "my beautiful wife what has happened that gave you this great joy, has the gods blessed your womb with my desired male child"? The wife responded "the one the gods has blessed us with is doing exceptionally well at school" and Afiangbe expected her husband to rejoice as well, Mr. Enoma responded with a hiss and said "is that one a child"? Please go get me my food and tell me something else. Afiangbe turned back angrily to get the food.

Inspite of the prevailing hatred of her father, Adesuwa remained focus and dedicated to her studies. After some years, Adesuwa was done with her Nursery 1-3 came out 1st in her class, after which she got prepared for her primary school.

CHAPTER THREE

ADESUWA RECIPOCATED WITH LOVE AND PEACE

At this stage in the life of Adesuwa, she was set to begin her primary school education and she was only 9 years old. She has grown to be a beautiful young lady Inspite of her adversity and ordeal she experienced at the very early stage of her life. In her area in Aduwawa, Benin City, Adesuwa was known generally as a polite and good girl. Inspite of the popularity of her Dad in the neighborhood, she greet people politely, go on errands for her elders, assist the mother in the kitchen as well as combine all these with her studies.

It is about time to begin her primary school education and her biggest challenge is how to get the finances to begin because she is fully aware that her dad will not be willing to assist her. Afiangbe came knocking again to her husband, you have kept quiet about our daughter, you are fully aware that it is time for her resume primary school, all her mates are done with their shopping for books, bags, sandals and other stuff to begin, what is your

plan for our own daughter Adesuwa. As this
conversation is going on, Adesuwa the
interested party involved was listening and was
anticipating a good response from her dad due
her good grades in her nursery years. Enoma
responded bluntly with anger saying "woman I
understand you have a business, if you so love
our daughter as you claim why not go ahead
and train her, because I am not spending any
penny on her this time around instead I will
keep all my resources until the gods will bless
me with a male child. Afiangbe left the husband
in tears and wondered why such hatred for
their daughter all because she is female.
Adesuwa also left disappointed and discourage.

The next day, Adesuwa met her dad in the
morning and greeted him cordially but got an
unfriendly respond. Adesuwa moved to her dad
room, packed some dirty clothes and began
wash them, cleaned the room and bath room,
dust the shoes and ensure everywhere was tidy.
After which she joined the mother in the
kitchen. Adesuwa told the mother, I heard your
conversation with dad yesterday why does
daddy hate me this much? What are my sins?
Did I chose to come into this world as female or
the gods predestined our sex? Afiangbe

consoled the daughter saying "it is not your fault, you have not committed any sins, you are a blessed child and I know one day your dad will retract his step and love you well, don't be discouraged, remain focused in life my daughter one day the gods will show you love and everyone will rejoice with you". Adesuwa responded with a smile and full of hopes. Afiangbe assured the daughter that she would try her possible best to ensure she begins school (primary 1) with her mates.

CHAPTER FOUR

ENOMA STILL WAITING ON THE GODS

Enoma lack the understanding that the gods are wise and that the gods give to you what they deem good for you per time. Enoma on this faithful day upon returning from the farm sat outside his house with his hands on his jaw questioning the gods. After 9 years they gave birth to Adesuwa, the Gods had not blessed them yet with another. The long anticipated male child is yet to come as he was pondering and crying to the gods, his friend Obaseki walked in. Obaseki asked him, what is wrong my friend did you lost any of your loved one? Did somcone harvest your crops from your farm? Talk to me what is the problem. Enoma responded with Anger "Obaseki I need a male child, who will carry this great legacy from one generation to another, who will inherit all my houses, my lands, and other properties I have acquired over the years.

Obaseki with a good heart tries to console his friend saying "the gods sees the heart, they will be blessed you as at the time that pleases them, you can't force them to do what is right, the time of the gods is always right my friend" Enoma responded angrily saying you are here talking because you already have two male children, today they followed you to the farm, they assist you a lot, you are a happy man advising me here like a baby. I need a male child urgently, please gods of our land hear my cry, Enoma continued in tears. Afiangbe returned from the market and met the husband in the distressed mode, she joined Obaseki to console the husband, saying all will be well, things will fall into places for us because I know the gods are wise and are not dead. Obaseki ignored the plea and continue to languish in penury and pains.

CHAPTER FIVE

THE IGUE FESTIVAL

The king of Benin Empire Oba Ewuare was a nice ruler over his people because of his philanthropist gesture and the love he showered on his people. Oba Ewuare was a warrior with large foot soldiers that conquered a lot of cities including Akure, Owo and other neighbouring towns to the Benin Empire. The reign of Oba Ewuare marked the beginning of the Igue festival which is celebrated as a festival to renew Oba Ewuare's magical powers. During the Igue ritual season, the Oba is prohibited from being in the presence of any non-native person. During the celebration of the Igue festival, it is forbidden to hold any burial or funeral ceremonies in Benin kingdom. This is because Igue is seen as a period of joy, and should not be interrupted with any form of public mourning.

The king Oba Ewuare announced via his town criers that to mark the end of the Festival is a dance competition for all the maidens of the land age 9-15 years of age and the winner will be going home with a cash price. The announcement made every young girl in Benin Empire joyful and there is hope of winning a price after the festival. Young girls formed groups and were practicing all over the town because they know the price will be given to the very best among them.

Afiangbe quickly intimated the daughter Adesuwa of the good news and advised her to key into it, who know the gods may favour her. Afiangbe bought a dress and a shoe as well as well decorated beads to make Adesuwa beautiful and exceptional. On the day of the dance competition, Adesuwa was getting dressed and prepared for the highly anticipated event the dad Enoma saw her and said "Adesuwa you want to go there and waste your time, like I always told you nothing good can come out from you, you are a total waste. Adesuwa cried and ran inside feeling very sad, the mum encourage her to be motivated as her sole aim now is to win the prize.

CHAPTER SIX

THE DANCE COMPETITION BEGINS

The day of the dancing competition had finally come and there were a lot of beautifully maidens ready to partake in the highly anticipated event. Over a hundred girls applied to be part of the competition, because of the great number the competition was scheduled to hold for two days and Adesuwa was schedule for the second day.

The Iyase of Benin who is the Second in Command to the Oba, Prime Minister, Commander in Chief of ancient Benin empire military, declared the dance ceremony open on behalf of the Oba. The head of the Benin cultural group were fully there to assess the dancers and pick the best among them. The first day witnessed a lot of good performances from the dancers as they all did their best to impress the judges. Five (5) dancers were selected from the fifty 50 that partook in the dancing for the first day. On the second day, Adesuwa woke up and cried to the gods for favour, she cried saying "Ogun my god of war, my god of battle, assist me in this competition and I will worship you forever".

When it was morning, the drums started and the cultural group sang some epic Benin songs and the dancing began. When it was the turn of Adesuwa, the gods smile on her as she danced effortlessly to the best of her abilities. She was favoured and announced to be among the best five (5) dancers of the second day. The Oba, chiefs and other prominent men present there immediately congratulated Mr Enoma for the daughter's epic performance; he pretended to smile because he still felt nothing good could come out of the daughter Adesuwa. While the women there rushed to the mother to celebrate with her on the performance of Adesuwa. The third day was fixed for the final day of the dancing competition to select one (1) out of the 10 best dancers selected from the first and second day of the competition.

On the third day of the competition, Adesuwa went there full of hope, with her eyes focused on the prize, it was indeed a life changing opportunity for her to cling the prize. Adesuwa was the fifth to dance on that faithful day; she performed wonderfully beyond all reasonable doubt. The head of the Benin cultural group after careful deliberation with other panel of judges announced Adesuwa the winner, a cash prize of 50 cowries was immediately presented to Adesuwa which was received happily by her mother Afiangbe. There was wide jubilation because everyone wished Adesuwa to win because of her performance.

When Adesuwa got home, the mum showered her with praises and thank the gods for the favour. Adesuwa needed just 5 cowries to begin school; she received a cash gift of 50 cowries meaning there is full hope and assurance of starting school immediately.

CHAPTER SEVEN

ADESUWA BACK TO SCHOOL

Adesuwa was joyful and happy; she went back on her knees to thank the gods for making her the winner. The dad saw her in the morning and answered her greetings casually without congratulatory messages. Adesuwa resumed school strong and focused on becoming the best in her class. She resumed 2 weeks behind the scheduled date of resumption. Her colleagues and friends were so delighted to receive her in school.

Adesuwa was so popular among her peers as the winner of the dancing competition, her name rang bell across the school, as she was known also by teachers and school management. Adesuwa moved around with dignity with her head and shoulder raised high as she is known all over the Benin Empire as a great dancer that won the enviable price of 50 cowries. In class Adesuwa was very attentive, answered questions frequently and she ensured her presence was felt in the school.

Adesuwa's mum Afiangbe was very delighted that her beloved daughter had finally resumed school just like her mates, as she have always wished for her daughter to have quality education.

CHAPTER EIGHT

Adesuwa Aging Gracefully

After several years, Adesuwa have grown to be a very beautiful lady at age 15. Mr. Enoma welcomed a new neighbor into their second flat named Justice who was a road worker from Benue State. Mr Justice was in his middle age and still not married. Mr. Enoma tried to enquiry from Mr Justice why he is still single at 45 years, he laughed saying he was searching and waiting for the right one. As they were talking and laughing, Adesuwa walked in with food prepared for the dad which is black soup with bush meat and pounded yam with a very nice aroma. Mr. Justice inquired quickly, is this beautiful damsel your daughter, and Mr. Enoma responded Yes. Mr. Justice responded swiftly, thanks be unto the gods for I have found my wife. Mr. Enoma was glad and willing to marry off her daughter to middle aged man not minding her education or consent.

CHAPTER NINE

Adesuwa Disagreed with Father Decision

Mr Enoma met the wife and discusses his intention to give Adesuwa hand in marriage to Mr Justice. The wife was against the decision and said she love the daughter to finish her education and become successful in Life. Inspite of the resistance, Mr. Enoma told Mr Justice come with his kinsmen to take Adesuwa after the traditional marriage rite. Due to the pressure on Adesuwa by the Dad, she ran away from home and stayed outside there she met some Christian missionaries spreading the gospel of Christ from the United Kingdom, they promised to help her. They went to Mr. Enoma to speak to him instead he refused and said the daughter must get married immediately. They left and promised to take Adesuwa back to the United Kingdom.

CHAPTER TEN

Adesuwa Followed the Missionaries

Adesuwa followed the missionaries and was granted Asylum and stay in the United Kingdom. Upon finishing her secondary school she was granted scholarship to study law in the United Kingdom.

Upon graduation, Adesuwa was attached as a Legal Adviser to the royal family. Adesuwa was highly loved and supported by the royal family. Adesuwa was away from Benin kingdom for almost 6 years now and wished to return home because she knew her mum will be almost depressed missing her. After several pleas to her employer the Queen of England, her request was granted to visit her parents in Africa and the royal private yet was also approved to take her home with some high power delegation.

CHAPTER ELEVEN

Adesuwa Returned Home in a Big Way

Adesuwa returned home, the private jet landed in Benin, everyone was glad that there lost daughter is back home alive in a higher level. She was led to the Oba palace of Benin. The news went round that there is a visitor in the Land. Mr. Enoma, the wife Afiangbe all ran to the palace to see who the royal visitor was that came to their land on a private yet with a high powered delegation.

Getting to the palace Mr. Enoma met the daughter looking great receiving royal treatment in the palace. Getting there, the mum shouted Adesuwa my daughter, they rushed and hugged each other in Tears. Mr. Enoma was scared to come close to the daughter due to the sufferings and ordeals she put him through while growing up.

Mr. Enoma cried in a loud voice saying "a girl child is important after all". Adesuwa forgive the dad and he made an announcement in the palace and advised all men that "Love and care for your girl child, show them love, educate them, they are also an asset like their male counterparts".

Adesuwa built a lot of water boreholes to ensure the kingdom have portable drinking water and showed love the parents. She also established an NGO in Benin to cater and support girl children before traveling back to continue her assignment with the queen of England and lived in affluence ever after. She later sent invitation to the parents to visit the United Kingdom and they lived happily and enjoyed a good life.